Put Beginning Readers on the F
ALL ABOARD READI

The All Aboard Reading series is especially designed ... ...ginning readers. Written by noted authors and illustrated in full color, these are books that children really want to read—books to excite their imagination, expand their interests, make them laugh, and support their feelings. With fiction and nonfiction stories that are high interest and curriculum-related, All Aboard Reading books offer something for every young reader. And with four different reading levels, the All Aboard Reading series lets you choose which books are most appropriate for your children and their growing abilities.

Picture Readers
Picture Readers have super-simple texts, with many nouns appearing as rebus pictures. At the end of each book are 24 flash cards—on one side is a rebus picture; on the other side is the written-out word.

Station Stop 1
Station Stop 1 books are best for children who have just begun to read. Simple words and big type make these early reading experiences more comfortable. Picture clues help children to figure out the words on the page. Lots of repetition throughout the text helps children to predict the next word or phrase—an essential step in developing word recognition.

Station Stop 2
Station Stop 2 books are written specifically for children who are reading with help. Short sentences make it easier for early readers to understand what they are reading. Simple plots and simple dialogue help children with reading comprehension.

Station Stop 3
Station Stop 3 books are perfect for children who are reading alone. With longer text and harder words, these books appeal to children who have mastered basic reading skills. More complex stories captivate children who are ready for more challenging books.

In addition to All Aboard Reading books, look for All Aboard Math Readers™ (fiction stories that teach math concepts children are learning in school) and All Aboard Science Readers™ (nonfiction books that explore the most fascinating science topics in age-appropriate language).

All Aboard for happy reading!

To Gwen, my own #1 soccer player—J.B.S.

For Yvonne and her three dogs—C.D.

Text copyright © 2003 by Judith Bauer Stamper. Illustrations copyright © 2003 by Chris Demarest. All rights reserved. Published by Grosset & Dunlap, a division of Penguin Putnam Books for Young Readers, 345 Hudson Street, New York, NY 10014. GROSSET & DUNLAP and ALL ABOARD MATH READER are trademarks of Penguin Putnam Inc. Published simultaneously in Canada. Printed in the U.S.A.

Library of Congress Cataloging-in-Publication Data

Stamper, Judith Bauer.
    Go, Fractions! / by Judith Bauer Stamper ; illustrated by Chris Demarest.
      p. cm. — (All aboard math reader. Station stop 3)
    Summary: The Fractions team is coached by a math teacher who helps them learn while they play to become "number one" in soccer. [1. Fractions—Fiction. 2. Mathematics—Fiction. 3. Soccer—Fiction.]
    I. Demarest, Chris L., ill. II. Title. III. Series.
    PZ7.S78612 Go 2003
    [Fic]—dc21

2002151246

ISBN 0-448-43113-0 (pbk)   A B C D E F G H I J
ISBN 0-448-43139-4 (GB)   A B C D E F G H I J

GO, Fractions!

By Judith Bauer Stamper
Illustrated by Chris Demarest

Grosset & Dunlap • New York

Chapter 1: Tryouts

It was Saturday morning. The kids were up early. Today was tryouts for the new soccer team.

Danny and Rosa walked to the field together.

"Oh, no," Rosa said. "Look at all the kids!"

"Everybody wants to play soccer," Danny said.

Rosa and Danny joined friends from their class.

"Do you think everybody will make the team?" Kate asked.

"I hear they cut half the kids who try out," Mike said.

"Wow," Danny said. "That would be one out of every two players!"

Just then, a loud whistle blew.

Everyone looked across the field.
A tall man walked toward them.

"It's the coach," Kate said.

"He's a teacher at the middle school,"
Mike said. "He teaches math."

The whistle blew again. The kids
stopped talking.

"I'm Coach Curtis," the man said.
He put down a big bag of soccer balls.

"Welcome to tryouts. First, I want you to line up and count off."

The kids lined up. Danny was first. He called out one. The last kid in line called out sixteen.

"Okay," Coach Curtis said. "Break into two groups. The first half of you come over here with me. The second half stay where you are."

Eight kids walked over to the coach. He gave them each a ball. He had them line up and face the other players.

"Pass the ball to one another," the coach said. "And remember, don't touch the ball with your hands . . . just your feet!"

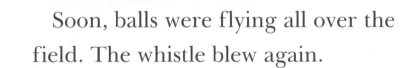

Soon, balls were flying all over the field. The whistle blew again.

"Next," Coach Curtis said. "I want a fourth of you to kick goals. The rest of you can keep passing the ball."

"A fourth of us?" Mike whispered. "How many is that?"

"Half of us is eight," Rosa said. "And a fourth is half of a half. So that would be four."

Danny led the first four players to the goal. Coach Curtis stood inside the net. He rolled the ball to Danny and told him to kick it—hard!

Danny aimed for the right corner of
the net. He gave the ball a hard kick.
It whizzed right past the coach's hands.

"Goal!" the kids yelled.

Everyone took a turn kicking a goal.
Soon, all sixteen players had given it a try.

Next, Coach Curtis had everyone run up and down the field. Rosa ran the fastest.

Coach Curtis blew his whistle. "Gather round," he ordered. "Tryouts are over."

The kids stood in a circle around him. "Any questions?" he asked.

"How many of us will you cut?" Mike asked in a nervous voice.

A big smile came over the coach's face. He pulled out a pile of shirts from his bag. "I have sixteen shirts. And sixteen players. You're all on the team!"

A cheer went up. Danny and Rosa gave each other a high five.

"What's our team's name?" Kate asked.

"The Fractions," Coach Curtis said. "I'm a math teacher, you know. And I love fractions!"

The coach handed out the shirts one by one. On the backs were numbers. But they were fractions!

Danny got ½. Rosa was ¼. Kate was ⅔. And Mike got ¾.

"Okay, team," Coach Curtis said. What's your name?"

"The Fractions!" the kids yelled.

"And what's your game?" the coach asked.

"Soccer!" the kids yelled.

"And what number do you want to be?" the coach yelled.

The kids all looked at each other for a minute. Then they yelled it out together.

"Number one!"

Chapter 2: Practice

The Fractions all came to practice after school the next Monday. They wore their team T-shirts with their fraction numbers.

"²/₃," Coach Curtis yelled to Kate. "Get over here in the goal. I want to see you make some saves."

Kate ran to the goal. She crouched down, ready to catch the ball.

"½," Coach Curtis yelled to Danny. "See if you can get a ball past her."

Kate stopped Danny's first three tries. But he got the fourth ball past her into the net.

"Good work, goalie," the Coach told Kate. "You stopped ¾ of his kicks!"

Team Roster

Danny 1/2
Rosa 1/4
Kate 2/3
Mike 3/4
Trish 1/3
Ethan 1/8
Hannah 3/8
Andrew 1/10

The rest of the kids got busy dribbling the ball and passing it to one another. Everyone worked hard for 45 minutes. Then Coach Curtis blew his whistle.

"It's time for a break," the coach said. "First, I want each of you to drink plenty of water. I have cups and a jug of water on the bench."

The kids ran over to the water. They each drank two cups full.

"Now sit down and take a rest, kids," the coach said. "Before we start practice again, I want to talk fractions."

Coach Curtis paused and looked around. His eyes came to rest on Mike. "Mike, what is a fraction?" he asked.

"A fraction is part of a bigger whole," Mike answered.

Everyone stared at Mike in amazement.

"I asked my older brother," Mike explained. "Coach Curtis is his teacher in middle school."

"Good work, Mike," the coach said. "Now who can tell me which is bigger— ½ or ¼?"

"It must be ¼," Rosa guessed. "Because 4 is bigger than 2."

"No, ½ is bigger than ¼," Danny said.

"I think Rosa is right," Kate said.

"I think Danny is right," Mike said.

"No arguments," Coach Curtis said. "Let's find out the correct answer by cutting apart some oranges."

"Can we eat the oranges, too?" Mike asked.

"Only after we finish talking about fractions," Coach Curtis said.

The coach reached into his red cooler and pulled out eight oranges and a knife. He sat the oranges on top of a table beside his flip chart.

"Okay, here is one whole orange," the coach said. He picked up an orange and then drew one on the flip chart.

"Now I'm going to cut the orange into two equal parts. What is each part called?"

"A half," Danny called out. "Just like my number!"

Coach Curtis cut the orange in two and drew a line through the middle of the orange on the flip chart.

"Now I'm going to cut another orange in half and then into half again. What do I call these parts?"

"Fourths," Rosa said. "You have ⁴⁄₄."

"Okay, kids," Coach Curtis said,
holding up ½ an orange and ¼ of an
orange. Which fraction is bigger—
a ½ or a ¼?"

"Danny was right," Rosa said.
"½ is bigger than ¼."

"Okay, Fractions," Coach Curtis said, "remember this rule: the larger the bottom number of a fraction is, the smaller each part is. Got it?"

"Got it," Mike said. "But I'm hungry! Can I have half an orange?"

"Everyone gets half an orange," the coach said. "But you have to make a choice. You can have one piece that is ½ an orange or you can have 2 pieces that are each ¼ of an orange. Which choice do you want?"

For a minute, everyone was quiet. They just stared at the oranges.

Finally, Kate shouted out. "$\frac{1}{2}$ and $\frac{2}{4}$ are the same!"

Coach Curtis laughed. "That's right, Kate. Now I have just three more questions before we eat. Here's the first: What's your name?"

"The Fractions!" everyone yelled.

"And what's your game?" the coach
asked.

"Soccer!"

"And what number do you want to be?"

"Number one!"

Chapter 3: The Big Game

"Okay, team," Coach Curtis said. "Today is the big day."

"Our first game!" Rosa added.

"Tell me, Fractions," the coach said. "Are we going to win?"

"You bet!" all sixteen members of the team yelled.

"Look," Danny shouted, "Here comes the other team!"

All eyes turned to the parking lot. A
school bus pulled in and came to a stop.
Sixteen kids piled out of the bus. They
all wore yellow shirts with black stripes.
The shirts said TIGERS.

"The Tigers," Kate whispered to Mike.
"That sounds kind of scary!"

"Let's go, team," Coach Curtis said.
"Get out on the field and show them
how good you are!"

The Fractions ran onto the field to
warm up. They passed the ball back and
forth. They practiced kicking goals.

Suddenly, a loud whistle blew. A referee in a black-and-white uniform came onto the field.

"Game time is in one minute," the referee said. "The Tigers won the toss. They'll start with the ball."

Coach Curtis gathered the Fractions together.

"Kate, you're in goal," he said. Then he counted off ten more players. "You ten get out on the field in your positions. The rest of you be ready to go in as substitutes."

The Fractions lined up against the Tigers. The referee blew her whistle. The game was on!

One of the Tigers passed the ball right by Danny. It was too fast for him to stop! The Tigers moved the ball closer and closer to the Fractions' goal. Then one of the Tigers gave the ball a hard kick. It whizzed right past Kate into the net!

"Goal!" the Tigers shouted.

Kate stamped her foot on the ground. She was angry at herself.

"We'll get it back, Kate," Danny yelled. "Don't worry!"

Danny brought the ball down the field for the Fractions. But he didn't get very far. The Tigers were good. They stole the ball away.

But Kate didn't let another Tiger ball
get into the goal. She stopped five of
their shots.

At halftime, the referee blew her whistle.
The Fractions dragged over to the bench.

"I'm beat!" Mike said.

"I've never run so much in my life!"
Rosa said.

"Sit down and rest," Coach Curtis said.
"Drink some water. I'm going to send
in five fresh players. Half of the ten field
players can stay here and rest. The other
half has to go back in."

"I'll stay on the bench," Emily said. "I
hurt my ankle."

Four other kids said they wanted a rest.

"Kate, I want you back in goal," Coach Curtis said. "You're doing a great job!"

"How much more time is left in the game?" Mike asked.

"Our games last 60 minutes," the Coach said. "And it's halftime now. So how long do we have left to play?"

"30 minutes," the team yelled.

"Let's make them great!" Coach Curtis said.

The Fractions ran back on the field, giving one another high fives. The Tigers came back on the field acting like they owned it.

The referee blew the whistle. Danny started to dribble the ball down the field. But a Tigers player stole it right away from him.

"Oh no you don't!" Danny said. He stuck his foot in and stole the ball right back. He passed it to Mike. Mike passed it back to Danny. They worked the ball down to the Tigers' goalie. Then Danny made a fake to the left. But he hit the ball to the right! It sailed right into the back of the goal!

"Score!" Coach Curtis yelled. The Fractions on the bench all jumped up and yelled. The players on the field crowded around Danny and cheered.

"The game is tied, 1 to 1," Rosa said. "But we haven't won yet!"

The Tigers got the ball. They looked determined. They passed the ball down the field until they were right near Kate and the Fractions' goal.

One of the Tigers started for the goal. Mike ran right in front of him and knocked him down.

The referee blew her whistle. "Penalty kick," she yelled.

"Oh, no," Mike said. "I didn't mean to do that!"

"Make a wall," Coach Curtis yelled.

The Fractions lined up in a wall in front of Kate and the goal. The Tigers player kicked the ball at the goal. It sailed high in the air, right toward the back of the net. Kate made a huge jump into the air. She caught the ball!

The Fractions took over the ball. Danny and Rosa passed it back and forth down the field.

From the sidelines, Coach Curtis yelled out, "Only five more minutes!"

Danny came close to the goal. But he knew the goalie was watching him. He acted like he was going to kick. But, instead he passed the ball to Rosa.

Rosa gave the ball a hard boot. It shot right past the Tigers' goalie. It hit the back of the net!

"Goal!" Danny yelled.

The Fractions jumped up and down with joy.

"There are two minutes left!" Coach Curtis yelled. "You haven't won yet!"

The Tigers tried to take the ball down the field. But the Fractions fought them off.

The final whistle blew. The game was over!

Coach Curtis and the rest of the
Fractions ran out onto the field.

"What's your name?" the coach asked.

"The Fractions!" the kids yelled back.

"And what's your game?" the coach
asked.

"Soccer!" the kids yelled.

"And what number are you?' Coach
Curtis asked with a big smile.

"We're Number one!" The Fractions
yelled. "NUMBER ONE!"